Barney The Lighthouse

Written by Heidi Aigler
Illustrated by Zach Wideman

Barney The Lighthouse

Text and Illustrations:
Copyright © 2016 Heidi Aigler. All rights reserved.

Story and Script:
Heidi Aigler

Illustrations and Graphic Design/Layout:
Zach Wideman, www.widemanillustrations.com

**For Jim and Shirley,
who first showed me the light.** - H.A.

**And for Gordie,
the lighthouse enthusiast.** - Z.W.

Barney was a very tall lighthouse on the edge of the sea. He stood with his red top and his white bottom, and shone his bright light into the sky. All the ships, and all the birds, and all the visitors to Long Beach Island could see Barney's light from miles away.

Barney shone his light on clear nights
to guide the fishing boats home.

"Hello Mr. Ritter!" Barney said as Mr. Ritter and his fishing boat chugged through the inlet.

"Hello Barney!" called Mr. Ritter from the pilot house. "Thank you for lighting my way home."

Barney shone his light on foggy nights to warn
the cargo ships away from the rocks. The cargo
ships carried books and toys for good little girls
and boys.

"Watch out Captain Jim, you are very close to shore!" called Barney.

"Thank you Barney! We almost sailed right into the beach," called Captain Jim, as he sailed away from the shore and safely out to sea.

But Barney's favorite job was to let visitors climb the many, many stairs inside him all the way to the top. The visitors walked around his top, high up in the sky, and could see far, far away.

"Hee hee hee! Ha ha ha!" laughed Barney, as the visitors climbed up and down his insides.

"That tickles!"

One dark night, a huge storm rolled in from the sea. The rain lashed Barney's red top and white bottom. The thunder rumbled Barney's windows. The wind blew all around him. The storm shattered Barney's light, and the sea grew even darker.

The next day, Mr. Ritter saw Barney's broken light. And there were no fish that day.

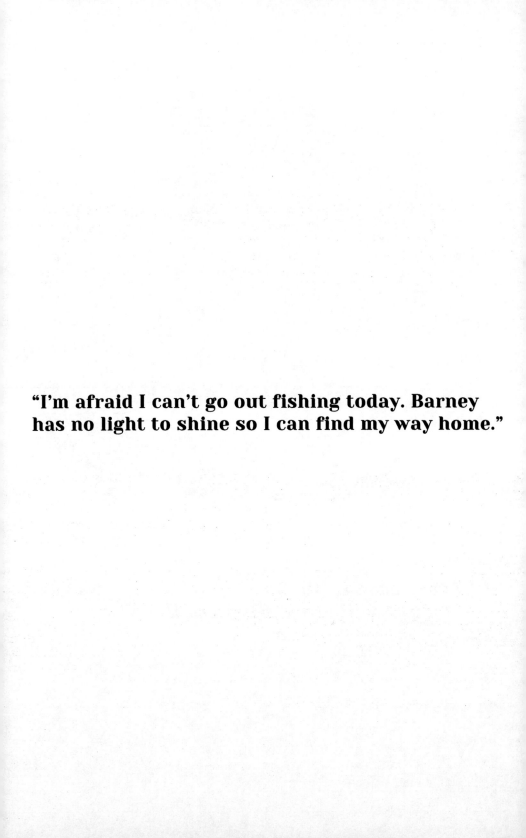

"I'm afraid I can't go out fishing today. Barney has no light to shine so I can find my way home."

The cargo ships couldn't see the shore without Barney's bright light. There were many sad boys and girls that day.

"Oh no!" cried Captain Jim, "Our ship is stuck on the rocks. How will we ever deliver our toys?"

It wasn't safe for visitors to climb up and down Barney's stairs with the broken glass from the light. "We drove all day to see the sea from the top of Barney's tower!" cried the visitors. And they went back home disappointed.

Everyone on Long Beach Island looked up at
Barney's broken light and was sad. But Fireman
Joe knew what to do. So Fireman Joe bought
a new light from the lighthouse store, and
carried it up, up, up all the stairs to Barney's
top. He took out the old broken light, swept
up the broken glass, and put in the new light.
It shone brighter than ever.

"Why, all we have to do is replace Barney's light, and he'll be as good as new!" he said with a smile.

The next day, Mr. Ritter went out in his fishing boat again. Barney's light was shining once more to show him the way home. Everyone had delicious fish for dinner that evening.

"Good night Mr. Ritter!" caled Barney.

"Goodnight Barney! It's good to see your light again!" called Mr. Ritter.

The cargo ship carrying toys saw Barney's light shining, and Captain Jim steered away from the shore. All the good little boys and girls once again got their toys.

"No hitting the rocks today!
Thank you Barney!" said Captain Jim.

And the visitors could once again climb, climb, climb up all Barney's steps, and look far, far, far out across the sea. All the visitors smiled, and Barney laughed at the tickling feeling from the people inside him.

**And Barney is still shining his light tonight.
Goodnight Barney!**

I hope you enjoyed reading my story! Did you notice my little bird friend? He's always around. Go back to the beginning of the story and see if you can find him on every page!

A Note To Readers

Barney the Lighthouse is based on a real lighthouse in New Jersey built on the real Long Beach Island. The Barnegat Lighthouse is located in the town of Barnegat Light. Visitors can walk up the many, many stairs to the top of the lighthouse, just like in the book! If you loved reading about Barney, be sure to make a trip to New Jersey to see it in person. Photo courtesy of James Lake.

Made in the USA
San Bernardino, CA
02 May 2016